**This Little Tiger
book belongs to:**

_____

_____

T0386757

LITTLE TIGER PRESS LTD,
an imprint of the Little Tiger Group
1 Coda Studios, 189 Munster Road, London SW6 6AW
Imported into the EEA by Penguin Random House Ireland,
Morrison Chambers, 32 Nassau Street, Dublin D02 YH68
www.littletiger.co.uk
First published in Great Britain 2022
Text by Danielle McLean
Text copyright © Little Tiger Press Ltd 2021
Images used under license from Shutterstock.com
Incidental artwork by Michelle Lancaster
All rights reserved • ISBN 978-1-80104-236-9
Printed in China • LTP/2700/4364/1021
2 4 6 8 10 9 7 5 3 1

CRAZY STICKERS

CREATE-A-DINOSAUR

LITTLE TIGER

LONDON

GAME ON!

> ... and then it hit me!

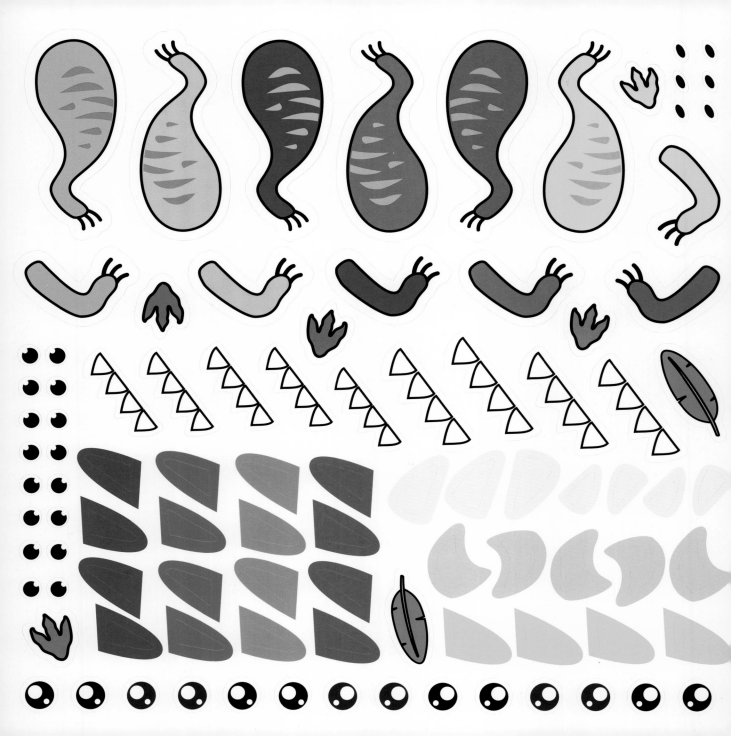

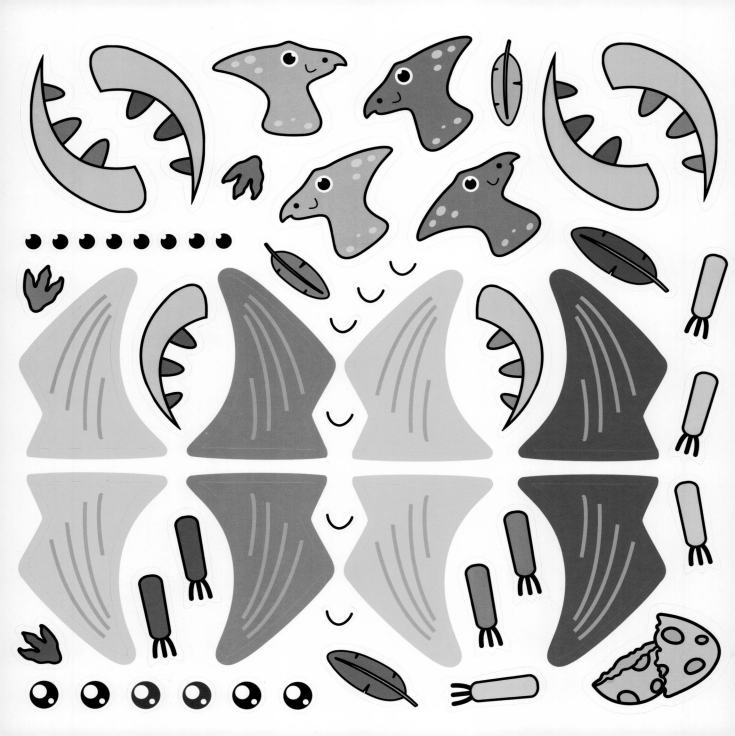

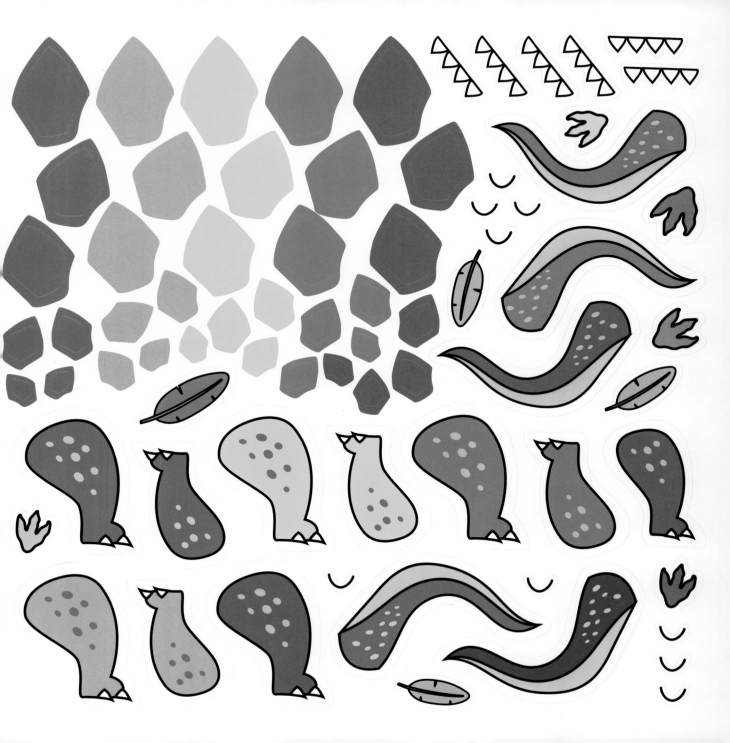

SWEET TREAT

No one stacks up to you!

Collect them all:

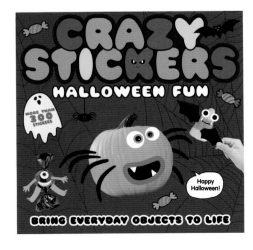